Dear Jo,
We love you
so much!!
Happy Birthday
from
Nana & Papa
xxxx
2024

Pearl

THE PROPER UNICORN

SALLY ODGERS

ILLUSTRATED BY
ADELE K THOMAS

FEIWEL AND FRIENDS   NEW YORK

For Imogen Grace. — SALLY ODGERS

To Maik, I wouldn't be able to do this without you.
Thank you. xxx — ADELE K THOMAS

A FEIWEL AND FRIENDS BOOK
An imprint of Macmillan Publishing Group, LLC
120 Broadway, New York, NY 10271

Our books may be purchased in bulk for promotional, educational, or business
use. Please contact your local bookseller or the Macmillan Corporate and
Premium Sales Department at (800) 221-7945 ext. 5442 or by email at
MacmillanSpecialMarkets@macmillan.com.

Library of Congress Control Number: 2020911162

ISBN 978-1-250-23554-1 (hardcover) / ISBN 978-1-250-23555-8 (ebook)

Feiwel and Friends logo designed by Filomena Tuosto

Originally published in 2019 in Australia by Scholastic Australia under the title
Pearl the Proper Unicorn.

First US edition, 2021

10 9 8 7 6 5 4 3 2 1

mackids.com

Chapter 1

It was a sunny morning in the Kingdom and Pearl was practicing her magic.

Making magic was easy for Pearl.
But making the *right* magic was not
so easy. Still, she was the only magical
unicorn in the Kingdom and her
friends, Olive and Tweet, loved it when
she made treats for them to share.

"yummy!"

Olive was an ogre. She laughed a lot
and she ate a lot, and if there was a
problem, Olive knew how to fix it.

Tweet was a firebird.
She was small, but she
could fly very fast.

"HMMM,"

Together, the three friends could do just about anything.

"I'll make pink strawberry pops today," Pearl said. "I'll try hoppity-toss. Then I'll add stamp-stamp."

Hoppity-toss-stamp-stamp went Pearl.

Nothing happened.

"Popping parsnips!" Pearl said. She wiggled her head twice and stamped her hoof. Wiggle-wiggle-stamp.

Oops. A shower of pink roses tumbled out of the sky and hooked themselves in Pearl's mane. How had she made roses? She'd been trying to make strawberry pops!

At least they were pink and sweet.

Pearl shook her mane and swished her tail to get rid of the roses. Their sharp prickles kept them in place.

"Bumpy balloons!" Pearl stamped and wiggled her head as she swished her tail again. Stamp-wiggle-swish!

She looked up. No strawberry pops. No roses, either.

She was about to try again when
someone called her name.

"Pearl! Quick!"

It was Tweet. She zipped over the low
trees and into the meadow.

Tweet dived and landed on Pearl's
horn. Then Tweet lost her balance and
dangled upside down from her claws.

Pearl squinted at her upside-down
friend. "What's the matter, Tweet?"

"Come quick!" the firebird said.

"**Sizzling soup!** Is something wrong?" Pearl asked.

Tweet flipped into the air and zipped off like an arrow.

Pearl forgot all about strawberry pops and galloped after her tiny friend.

Pearl caught up with Tweet on top of a hill. "Where's Olive?" Pearl asked, peering around.

Olive popped out from behind a big tree. "Pearl, you're not going to believe this! Just look!" She pointed down at the path winding through Big Rock Valley.

"Hiccuping hippos!"

Pearl said.

It was another unicorn.

Chapter 2

The unicorn in the valley pranced along the path on shining hooves. Pearl couldn't believe it!

"Aren't you going to go down and meet him?" Olive asked.

"**Pickled plums**, of course I am," Pearl said. "But what will I say? I've never met another unicorn before. What if he doesn't like me?"

Olive gave Pearl a big ogre hug. "Why wouldn't he, Pearl? You're the nicest unicorn in the Kingdom."

"I'm the only unicorn in the Kingdom," Pearl said. "I mean, I was until now."

"Just go and say hello, the way you would to any friend. We'll come and say hello later," said Olive.

Pearl nodded. Then she took a deep breath and trotted off toward the path.

Down the hill she went, faster and faster. She couldn't wait to meet the new unicorn.

But Pearl was so excited, she didn't see the patch of mud on the ground.

"Sour strawberry pops!" Pearl cried as she tumbled down the hill. She came to a stop, right behind the new unicorn.

The unicorn peered down at Pearl.
"Pardon me, but proper unicorns never
tumble down hills," he said.

Pearl jumped to her feet. "I'm sorry."

The unicorn was white, with a blue
mane and the longest tail Pearl had
ever seen. His horn sparkled.

"Stop staring," the unicorn said. "Proper unicorns never stare."

"You're so—" Pearl was about to say beautiful, but instead she said, "I thought I was the only unicorn in the Kingdom."

The unicorn laughed. "I don't live here. I'm looking for an important quest."

"Ooh!" Pearl loved quests. She and Tweet and Olive always went on quests. "What kind of quest are you looking for?" she asked.

"I haven't found one yet. His Majesty King Primus the Proud sent me to look for one," the unicorn said.

Then he looked Pearl up and down. "Do you always wear roses in your mane?" he asked.

Pearl wasn't sure how to explain that her magic didn't always work, so she just nodded.

"My name is Prince Percival the Positively Perfect Prancer," the unicorn said proudly. "My friends call me Prince Percy."

"That's a beautiful name," Pearl said. "I'm just Pearl."

"That won't do," Prince Percy said. "Unicorns are special, so you need a special name. I'll call you Princess Pearl Pretty Pants."

Pearl looked behind her, confused. "But I'm not wearing any pants," she said.

"So, Princess Pearl Pretty Pants, what are you doing today?" Percy asked.

"I'm trying to make pink strawberry pops for my friends," she said.

Prince Percy smiled. "Splendid! Show me."

Right, Pearl thought. She took a
deep breath.

Hoppity-toss-stamp-stamp went Pearl.

Nothing happened.

Hoppity-toss-stamp-stamp she
went. Oh, why wasn't it working? She
stamped her hoof again. Stamp.

Then down fell two pink strawberry
pops right on top of Prince
Percy's nose.

PLONK!

"Thank you!" said Prince Percy. Then he picked up both of the strawberry pops in his teeth.

"But—" began Pearl as Percy crunched. "I made those for my friends, Olive and Tweet. Olive's an ogre and Tweet's a firebird, and they love strawberry pops."

"You can't be friends with an ogre and a firebird!" said Prince Percy. "It isn't proper."

It isn't? thought Pearl.

Chapter 3

Pearl tried to magic up some more strawberry pops for Olive and Tweet anyway.

Hoppity-toss began Pearl.

"That's wrong for a start," Prince Percy interrupted.

Pearl stopped. "What do you mean?"

"Princess Pearl, unicorns don't make magic by hopping around," Percy said.

"I do." Pearl tossed her head twice and swished her tail. Wiggle-wiggle-stamp!

More pink roses tumbled down.

Now Percy had roses in his mane, too.

Pearl thought he looked perfectly handsome. But Percy didn't think so.

"Oops," Pearl said.

Percy held his head high. "The rose goes," he said. Then all the roses disappeared!

Pearl jumped back in surprise. "How did you do that? You didn't stamp or swish or anything."

"That's proper magic," Percy said.
"All that prancing and swishing and
stamping is just silly. Proper unicorns
are never silly."

But Pearl loved being silly! It was one of her favorite things. She knew her magic didn't always work the way she wanted it to. Maybe Percy could help her? "Can you teach me?" she asked.

"Of course. Watch." Percy closed his eyes.

Pearl wondered if he was falling asleep, but after a few seconds, Percy opened his eyes again and said, "Clip, clop, pink lollipop."

A pink lollipop popped into view, sticking up from the grass like a huge pink flower.

Percy ate it.
"Yum," he said.
"Much better
than the ones
you made."

"**Toppling turnips!**" Pearl
said. "I've been trying to magic up
strawberry pops all afternoon. That
was so clever, Percy! It just popped up
like a flower."

"That's because I did it properly," said
Percy. "Now you try."

Then Pearl heard heavy footsteps stomping down the hill.

Percy paused. "What's that horrible noise?"

"That's Olive," Pearl said. "She'd love to see your magic."

"Show an ogre magic? I don't think so. If that ogre is coming, I'm going," Percy said.

"But you were going to teach me—"

"Meet me by the big rock when that ogre has gone," Percy said as he trotted away, his blue mane bouncing in the air and his tail flying in the wind.

Chapter 4

As she watched him leave, Pearl wasn't sure what to think about Prince Percival the Positively Perfect Prancer.

Olive stopped stomping and slid in the mud down the rest of the hill. Tweet flew behind her.

WHEE!

"Did we miss the unicorn?" Olive asked. "We brought him a welcome present." She held up a basket of apples, covered in mud.

46

"Unicorn run?" Tweet asked.

"He had to leave," Pearl said.

"What's he like?" Olive
asked as she took a
bite of a muddy apple.

"His name is Prince Percival the Positively Perfect Prancer," Pearl explained.

Olive sighed. "Prince Percival the Positively Perfect Prancer. What a perfect name!"

"He calls me Princess Pearl Pretty Pants," said Pearl.

"Pretty Pants!" Tweet squawked, tumbling over on the ground. She giggled. "Pretty Pants . . ."

"So, when can we meet him?" Olive asked excitedly.

Pearl couldn't think of a polite way of saying Percy didn't want to be friends with a firebird and an ogre. Then she remembered. "He's looking for an important quest. And guess what? He's going to teach me to do proper magic!"

"You can do magic already, Pearl," said Olive, confused.

"Percy says I shouldn't swish my tail and stamp my hoof and toss my head. He says that's not proper."

"It's the way you do it, so it's perfectly proper," Olive said.

"Proper magic?" Tweet asked.

Pearl closed her eyes. "Lollipop," she said, because that had worked for Prince Percy.

She opened her eyes. Nothing happened.

Tweet and Olive looked at each other.

"Lollipop," Pearl said again.

Still nothing happened.

"Lollipop. Lollipop!" Pearl got so mad that she did a little hop, tossed her head, and stamped her hoof three times.

A small lollipop fell out of the sky.

"Yum!" Olive caught it in her hand and looked down at it.

"Very small," said Tweet.

"Still good," Olive said, taking a bite.

"**Jumping jellyfish!**" said Pearl. She hadn't made the lollipop appear the proper way. She had to have another lesson with Prince Percy if she was ever going to be a proper unicorn.

Chapter 5

Pearl was about to head back to Big Rock Valley to find Prince Percy when Tweet flew up and perched on her horn.

"Splash in pond?" she asked hopefully.

Pearl wanted to see Prince Percy, but splashing in the pond was one of her favorite things. The water was so cool and clear and the grass that grew around the banks was extra sweet and juicy.

"Let's go," Olive said.

Olive hopped up on Pearl's back and the
unicorn galloped happily up the hill.

Tweet flew off ahead of them. Pearl wondered if the firebird would pop out from behind a bush or drop a bunch of daisies on her head.

When they were almost at the pond, Pearl bounced to a stop.

"What's wrong?" Olive asked.

Pearl flicked her ear. "Can you hear
that noise?"

Olive listened with her ogre ears.
"I hear splashing."

Suddenly a scared Tweet shot toward them through the trees.

"Gobble-uns! Horrible gobble-uns!" she squawked.

Pearl laughed. "That's funny, Tweet."

"Not trick! Gobble-uns in pond!"

Pearl stared at her. "**Cackling cakes!**"

Quickly, Pearl, Olive, and Tweet raced toward the pond.

When they were close enough, the three friends stopped and peered through the bushes at the pond.

Three gobble-uns had set up camp by the pond. They were splashing around in the water. Usually the pond was clear and sparkling. Now it was the color of old pea soup.

Tweet pointed with her wing. "Told you!"

The smell of stinky magic made Pearl sneeze, but the gobble-uns had started singing, so they didn't hear her.

"Stinky wand,
Gobble-un pond!
Stink up the place,
For the gobble-un race!"

"Ugh," Olive said, wrinkling her ogre nose. "Look what they're doing!"

With each burst of stinky magic, the gobble-uns threw more stinky stuff into the pond.

It was too much for Olive. She jumped out of the bushes and stomped over to the edge of the pond. "Stop stinking up the pond!" she roared at the gobble-uns.

The gobble-uns laughed.

"It's OUR pond," said the biggest one. "We need stinky water to cook our stinky stew." He pointed a finger at a pot bubbling over a fire.

"It's everyone's pond," Pearl said, trotting over to stand next to Olive. Tweet followed, too.

The gobble-uns ignored her. The tallest one jumped out of the pond and started the others in a song.

"Go, ogre, go,
Or we'll stinkify your toe!
Go over there,
Or we'll stinkify your hair!"

He raised one arm to throw stinky magic at Olive.

"Sneaky socks!" cried Pearl. "Let's go!"

Olive, Pearl, and Tweet raced away from the pond as fast as they could.

"Magic?" Tweet asked Pearl.

"What about hoppity-swish-stamp? Would that work?" asked Olive.

Pearl was about to try when she remembered what Prince Percy had said. "That's not proper magic. Proper magic works every time."

"Try?" Tweet asked.

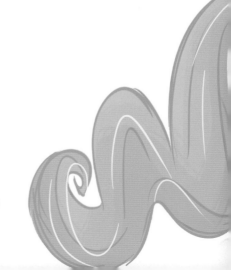

"Blundering bicycles!
Make gobble-uns go," Pearl said.

She waited. The gobble-un song continued. Pearl stamped her hoof twice and swished her tail, ending with a flick. Stamp-stamp-swish-flick!

"Yay!" yelled Olive as a horn tumbled from the sky and clonked on the ground. Olive picked it up, filled her lungs with air, put it to her lips, and blew.

PARRP!

It made the rudest noise Pearl had ever heard.

PARRP!
PARRP!

Tweet clapped her wings over her ears.

"Maybe this will scare the gobble-uns away," said Olive. "You're so clever, Pearl!"

"I wish we knew someone who could do proper magic . . ." said Pearl. Then she remembered—they did!

"Wait right here," Pearl said to Olive and Tweet. "I'm going to find Prince Percy!"

Pearl raced off through the meadow.

Chapter 6

Pearl galloped as fast as she could, straight to Big Rock Valley to find Prince Percy.

"Prince Percy?" Pearl called.

Prince Percy poked his head out from behind the rock. "Are you alone, Princess Pearl Pretty Pants? Are you here for your lesson? I can show you how to make a pink cupcake."

"Never mind cupcakes, Prince Percy. Come to the pond. I've found you a proper quest!"

"A quest!" said Prince Percy.

"I'll explain on the way!" said Pearl.
She galloped away from the big rock
and Prince Percy followed.

As they got near the pond, they
could hear Olive's horn.

PARRP!
PARRP!

Percy flicked his
perfect ears.
"What's that noise?"

"That's Olive and her
new horn," Pearl said.

PARRp! PARRp!

went Olive's horn again.

"Come on!" Pearl trotted closer.

Percy sniffed the air with his perfect nose. "There's a horrible smell, too."

"That's the gobble-uns!" Pearl explained.

"Ew! Gobble-uns!" said Percy in disgust.

"**Cackling carrots!** Prince Percy, getting rid of the gobble-uns is your important quest!"

Percy stopped. "I don't think so."

Pearl stared at him. "But my magic isn't the proper kind! Just come and meet Olive and Tweet."

When they found Olive and Tweet,
Olive bounced up and gave Pearl a
hug. Then she stomped toward Percy,
grinning.

Percy backed away.

"These are my friends, Olive and
Tweet," Pearl said.

"Lovely to meet you," Olive said in her politest voice. "Are you going to help us get rid of the gobble-uns in the pond?"

Tweet flew up. She tried to land on
Percy's head, but he moved away.

"Pearl said you do magic just like her,"
Olive said.

Percy tossed his mane. "I do proper
magic."

"You do it your way. Pearl does it her
way," Olive said.

"Just watch, Olive," said Pearl. "Percy will get rid of those gobble-uns."

Olive grinned and blew her horn. "Let's go, then."

Olive and Tweet raced toward the pond.

But Percy didn't move.

Pearl wanted to run after her friends, but she also wanted to get rid of the gobble-uns from the pond. She looked over at Prince Percy. What was she going to do?

Chapter 7

Pearl raced after her friends. She was happy to see that Prince Percy soon trotted behind her.

GOBBLE
-UN
POND

When they arrived, the gobble-uns were still being stinky. The pond was full of garbage, and the gobble-uns were cooking something horrible in the big pot.

"Stinky stew!
Stinky stew!
All for me,
None for you," they sang.

Then one of them turned and spotted
Pearl and Percy.

"Ooh, look! Let's make 'em stinky!"

The biggest gobble-un grabbed a
rotten turnip and threw it at Pearl.
It splattered all over her white coat.

"Get the other one!" howled the
big gobble-un.

The gobble-uns scooped up green glop
and threw it toward Percy.

Percy backed away. "Ew! Ew! Ew!"

"Do your proper magic," Pearl said.
"I'll stand in front of you so they don't
splatter you."

Pearl moved in front of Percy.
A mushy lettuce leaf hit her in the
face and dangled from her horn.
A squashed toadstool hit her shoulder.
More and more stinky things came
flying toward her.

"**Hopping hogs**, Percy! Say the words!" Pearl cried, ducking as a mushy mushroom came flying her way.

"Um . . . gobble-uns . . ." Percy began. "I—I can't think of a rhyme!"

"I can!" said Tweet.

Pearl and Percy looked up to see Tweet swoop into view above the trees.

"Wobble-un!" she cried.

That was it!

"Gobble-un! Wobble-un!" Pearl yelled.
She added a prance-flick-kick-wiggle-
hop as more sloppy gobble-un garbage
flew her way.

Suddenly the gobble-uns stopped throwing things. They froze, and then one of them wobbled. Another one fell against him. Soon they were all stumbling around.

"Wobble!" Tweet squawked.

The gobble-uns were wobbling all
right, but they weren't going away. One
of them wobbled right into the pond!

Pearl tried to think of some more
words to use, but all she could
remember were the lollipop words
Percy had used.

A stinky gobble-un wobbled toward
Percy and tangled his stinky fingers
in the unicorn's mane.

"Argh!" Percy cried. Then he turned and galloped away.

PARRp! The wobbling gobble-uns wobbled backward as Olive ran toward them, blowing her horn.

PARRP! PARRP!

Every time Olive blew the horn, the gobble-uns wobbled a few steps away.

Olive was blowing them back. Pearl gave up trying to think of rhymes. What could she do?

Aha! She remembered. Gobble-uns loved stink and hated pink! And Pearl knew just how to magic up something pink. Wiggle-wiggle-stamp.

A shower of prickly pink roses fell out of the sky and landed on the gobble-uns.

"Ugh! Pink! Yuck! Icky flowers!" The gobble-uns tried to get rid of the roses, but the prickles stuck to their clothes. Wiggle-wiggle-stamp.

More roses rained down,
sweetly scenting the pond.

PARRp! Olive blew her horn as loud as she could.

The gobble-uns stuck their dirty fingers in their ears and ran away, covered in roses.

Tweet swooped after them, giggling.
"Gobble-un, wobble-un! Pink stink!
Run run run!"

PARRp! Olive blew one last
blast and then put down the horn.
She grinned from ear to ear.

Pearl looked at the pond. It was still full of garbage and roses, but the gobble-uns had gone.

"**Jiggling jelly**, Olive, we did it!" Pearl said. "Tweet thought of the rhyme, and you blasted your horn."

"And you Covered them with roses," Olive said. She started to do the ogre stomp, her favorite dance.

"And I didn't do anything," Prince Percy said as he walked up to them, looking sad. "I'm sorry, Princess Pearl Pretty Pants. I just couldn't think of the proper words in a hurry."

"Your proper magic almost worked,"
Pearl said. "It just needed some help."

"From friends," Olive said. Then she
hugged Percy.

"Gobble-un run," Tweet said. "Wobble-
un, gobble-un." She walked along
Pearl's back, wobbling
and giggling.

Pearl sighed. "There's still a problem. The pond's all garbagey. I don't know how we're going to get it clean."

Percy raised his head. "Make the pond as clean as we've ever seen," he said.

And it worked! All the garbage disappeared!

"Cleaning the pond is a good quest," Pearl said.

"Yes . . . but I think I found something better," Percy said. "I found out there's more than one way to be a proper unicorn."

Pearl smiled.

Tweet giggled.

Olive blew her horn and continued
to dance the ogre stomp.

Pearl joined in. Hoppity-stamp-swish-
wiggle-swish!

Oops!

Pearl's magic had turned
Prince Percy's
blue mane . . .

. . . pink!

DON'T MISS PEARL'S OTHER MAGICAL ADVENTURES!

Pearl

THE MAGICAL UNICORN

SALLY ODGERS ♥ ADELE K THOMAS

Pearl

THE FLYING UNICORN

SALLY ODGERS ♥ ADELE K THOMAS

SALLY ODGERS was born in Tasmania, Australia, in 1957, and has lived there ever since. Sally began writing as a child, and her first book was published in 1977. More than 250 books have followed, including *Good Night, Truck*. She is married to Darrel Odgers, and they have two adult children, James and Tegan. Darrel and Sally live in a house full of books, music, and Jack Russell terriers.

SALLYODGERS.WEEBLY.COM

ADELE K THOMAS is a Melbourne-based illustrator, director, and art director with over ten years of design experience in animation production, TV, children's books, advertising, and apps.

ADELEKTHOMAS.COM